CUENTO
DE LUZ

For Silvia Flórez, who shines a light in the very darkest

places, and with the strength of her heart, makes the most

needy violets bloom.

To those who make their marks, hold out their hands and

fight for a better world in parts of Africa where children dream

of smiling once again.

- Ana Eulate

 **Vipeika**
Fundación

The author will donate all proceeds from
this book to the Vipeika Foundation.
www.fundacionvipeika.org

Life Is Beautiful!

Text © 2012 Ana A. de Eulate
Illustrations © 2012 Nívola Uyá
This edition © 2012 Cuento de Luz SL
Calle Claveles 10 | Urb Monteclaro | Pozuelo de Alarcón | 28223 Madrid | Spain
www.cuentodeluz.com
Original title in Spanish: ¡Bonita es la vida!
English translation by Jon Brokenbrow
ISBN: 978-84-15619-26-0
Printed by Shanghai Chenxi Printing Co., Ltd. in PRC, August 2012, print number 1300-03

FSC
www.fsc.org
MIX
Paper from
responsible sources
FSC® C007923

LIFE IS BEAUTIFUL!

Ana Eulate • Nívola Uyá

There's so much to learn, so much to discover, so many dreams to make come true...

Did you know that for every person, there's a giraffe with wings, ready to make you explore your country, your continent, your universe…but above all, your heart?

Did you know? Did you ever imagine it?

No?

Well, listen carefully to what happened one day to a little girl with big, big eyes in a far-off part of Africa.

"Are there *really* giraffes with wings?" thought Violet.

In fact, she'd actually seen one! Really! She'd even flown on its back! It was her very best friend. She closed her eyes to remember.

Violet lived in a little village in Kenya, close to the frontier with Uganda. There wasn't much nearby, just the usual things like goats, people with skin like hers (a dark chocolate color), not much food…

And her! **The giraffe with wings!**

She suddenly appeared one dark night when Violet's tummy was aching with hunger.

The giraffe with big eyes landed gently by her side, fanning Violet with its long eyelashes, and whispered into her ear:

"Climb onto my back, and I'll take you on a journey."

"But I can't," said Violet, "my family lives here."

"We'll be back in no time," said her new friend with the long, long neck. "Trust me."

Dawn was breaking.

They soared into the sky and flew over the little girl's village, which gradually shrank in size until it was tiny, like an ant's head.

"Everything looks so little!" she cried.

Violet, who only knew what was just within a few hours'
walk around where she lived, looked down at
everything excitedly.

Now she was really beginning to discover her homeland:

Africa.

The gentle wind wound her hair into even tighter curls.

Some elephants that were drinking and splashing in the water looked on in amazement as Violet and the giraffe glided over the enormous lagoon.

"Are you thirsty?" the giraffe asked Violet. "Let's drink some water."

They didn't just drink, but even swam in the water, and the giraffe with its long, graceful legs, nibbled on some delicious acacia leaves. The heat was suffocating.

The flamingos flapped their wings to welcome the pair. The breeze they created woke a lion that was sleeping nearby beneath the branches of a large tree, but he soon drifted back to sleep.

They flew over the wildlife, over the grassy plains, mountains, rivers, lakes and waterfalls. They looked down from the sky on the tropical rainforest, and even forests of bamboo and heather.

"My country is so beautiful! The plants and animals are amazing!" said Violet happily.

"You're right," said the giraffe, "but did you know that there are also places where the rainbow sometimes loses its colors when it sees that children are no longer smiling?"

Violet thought quietly to herself. Her friend's comment had made her feel very sad. "I know. But what can we do about it?" she asked.

"I have an idea," said the giraffe, blinking its eyes. "Asking people from other countries, near and far, who have more than us, to give us help." "But how can they do that? How could they help?" asked the little girl. "By collaborating, by working together, sharing their moments of happiness

and **seeds of love**, and by being generous," answered the giraffe. "And do you know what my other idea is, the most magical of all?"

"No, tell me, please! I really want to know!"

"Tickling everyone—tickling all of the children in all of the villages, in all parts of Africa. And even the grown-ups.

That's right! Millions and billions and trillions of tickles for the adults, and even the animals! Did you know that goats can't stop laughing when you tickle them? I've seen some in your village. We have to get them laughing, laughing until they cry.

Come on Violet, laugh! I'll tickle you with my eyelashes.

Flip, flap, flip flap! I want you to laugh for real!"

The little girl let out such a pure, clear laugh that the winged giraffe couldn't hold back a tear.

The little girl's laugh flew through space and turned into millions of tiny droplets of water that fell over the whole continent of Africa in an explosion of color. They turned into a huge rainbow that crossed from north to south and from east to west.

It watered the land, and everything turned green, filled with light, and filled with life.

And then, from the sky, they saw something incredible: people's **souls.** Violet had never seen them before! Because sometimes you have to fly high, high into the sky, a long way away, to see into the deepest part of human beings.

Shortly afterwards, when they had returned to Violet's village and before saying goodbye, the giraffe, her beautiful winged friend, told Violet a secret.

"You know, little girl with the big eyes, everyone, **everyone** without exception, children and grown-ups, of all the races on the earth, in every part of the world, has a winged giraffe that protects them. I want you to remember that, and carry it in your heart forever. All you have to do is to concentrate on your winged friend, the one we all have, ask them for help and they will appear, to take you on a journey.

A journey to explore your country, your continent and your universe…but above all, your heart.

"Remember, we'll see each other again very soon," said the amazing giraffe, the most incredible giraffe Violet had ever known, as it fluttered its eyelashes. "I have incredible hearing, and I can see things from a very, very long way away. I'll hear you and see you, however far away you are."

The little girl's face lit up with joy.

"And do you know something else?" asked the giraffe, waving its long, long neck. "You are very beautiful when you smile."

The little girl opened her enormous eyes, a huge smile spreading across her face, and replied,

"Beautiful? **It's life that is beautiful!**"